Jamie's a Hero

Jamie's a Hero

SUSANNE GERVAY

Illustrated by Cathy Wilcox

April 2001

To Merle
Kids are heroes
Susanne Gervay

📚 **Angus&Robertson**
An imprint of HarperCollins*Publishers*

To my wonderful sister,
Elizabeth, and our
children — S.G.

For Tim — C.W.

An Angus & Robertson Publication

Angus&Robertson, an imprint of
HarperCollins*Publishers*
25 Ryde Road, Pymble, Sydney, NSW 2073, Australia
31 View Road, Glenfield, Auckland 10, New Zealand

First published in Australia in 1994
Reprinted in 1994

National Library of Australia
Cataloguing-in-Publication data:

Gervay, Susanne.
  Jamie's a hero.
  ISBN 0 207 18590 5
  I. Title.
A823.3

Printed in Australia by McPherson's Printing Group, Victoria
6 5 4 3 2
97 96 95 94

Jamie's Almost a Hero

I'm trying to be a hero and I'm ten years old. My name is James, but Mum and Dad and my sister Victoria, call me Jamie.

There was a bad time in my life when I was ... a coward. I wouldn't stay overnight at my favourite cousins' house. I wouldn't play with friends without my mum there. I cried and had bad stomach aches when I went to school and WORST of all ... it's hard to tell you. I still have it a bit.

Mum says it's because she and Dad are divorced but they've been separated for ages. Well, I suppose I should tell you what the WORST is. I'll whisper it to you ... *I have the scariest nightmares*. Honestly, anyone would scream if they saw the disgusting gooey-eyed monsters sliming all over me.

I'm a real hero now though. I have a special job. Mum gave it to me. I have to look after my sister, Victoria. I know that sounds ordinary, boring and unhero-like. Wrong! You have to know my sister Victoria. Victoria is six years old with wavy brown hair that Mum puts into pigtails or sometimes a ponytail. Mum says she's beautiful and that she's a princess and Victoria really truly believes she's a princess. Once our cousin Roslyn said to Victoria that all grown-ups call kids princesses if they're girls. Victoria cried and cried. Later I asked Dad about that and he said that Mum would have to be a queen if Victoria was a princess. Or that Victoria would have to be married to someone in the royal family and Victoria wasn't even married. He'd laughed. I asked Mum about it. 'Jamie, she is a princess, because she's good and beautiful.'

'But Dad said that it's not true,' I told Mum.

'That's the problem with engineers. They're smart and can fix anything but they don't know about other things, like princesses. You know your father can't understand Santa Claus either. I think Santa Claus is important, don't you?' I nod, because I hope I'm getting a remote control four speed action car for Christmas.

'Jamie, the Santas we see in the shops at Christmas, they're just helpers. But there is a real Santa spirit. Can't you imagine Santa Claus at the North Pole spreading happiness to all his helpers to make children laugh at Christmas? You laugh at Christmas, don't you?'

'Yes, Mum.'

'Jamie, you understand Santa Claus, don't you?' I think a while. There must be a reason for all those helpers to be dressed in red suits with white beards. Why would all the grown-ups buy presents for children and sing carols and give Christmas cards with Santa and his reindeers on them?'

'Mum I do believe in Santa's spirit. I think Dad is sort of unlucky not to believe in Santa or princesses or anything magic.'

I'm different to Dad.

'When I'm grown-up and an inventor, I want to be an engineer inventor. But I want to believe in special things too.'

'You will, Jamie,' Mum says and she hugs me.

This still doesn't explain why I'm like a hero while minding my sister Victoria, does it? Well, Victoria has a real temper. She hits me when she can't get what she wants. When I was on the phone at Dad's place yesterday talking to Mum, she wanted to talk to Mum too. So what did she do? With her rotten fist she hit me on the ear as hard as she could. I couldn't help screaming in pain. My ear was red and throbbing. And she just picked up the receiver and started talking to Mum as if nothing had happened. I heard Mum saying on the phone that Victoria was a bad girl. She wasn't a princess then, if you ask me.

So I have a lot to put up with. But I still have to look after her, because she's little and gets into all

kinds of trouble, and she's my sister. Mum says that my sister and my cousins, Roslyn and Lennie, are the most important people in the world to me. When I'm grown-up they'll be my friends always.

I worry about growing up. I'm scared I'll pick the wrong person to marry.

I saved Victoria's life on Saturday. It was all on account of her bad temper. Mum'd given us money to buy some milk and an iceblock each at the corner shop. I was going to get an orange iceblock and Victoria wanted a red one. It's my responsibility to hold Victoria's hand when we cross the road. But she wouldn't hold my hand and shouted at me, 'No, I can do it myself,' and just started running across the road without looking. There was a giant red car coming around the corner. Luckily I think fast — you have to with a sister like her. I grabbed Victoria's shirt and pulled her away. The car screeched to a stop, missed her by a tiny, little bit. My sister, Victoria could have been dead.

Me, Jamie, hero, inventor extraordinaire saved, through quick thinking and bravery, my sister Victoria.

Jamie the Inventor

It's hard work being an inventor. The main problem is getting the material to use for my inventions. Mum tries her best, but she's not very good at getting the right stuff. It's on account of her being an English teacher. She's good at telling stories and making me understand things and making me braver, but hopeless at getting the right sized batteries for my tin can fan to work, or getting the right wire for my aluminium and nail crane. I have to wait till I go to Dad's to get the right stuff. He knows everything about inventing and science and chemistry. Dad bought me the best electricity experiment set. There are all these wires I attach to lights and batteries and circuits and it makes alarms and hearing aids. It's just the best. I leave it at his unit because he reckons Mum doesn't look after things. It's not true. Mum does. Anyway, Mum can't help it if Victoria comes into my room and wrecks things. Mum tells Victoria to stay out of my room.

I'm in luck. There's a Council throw-out. You

want to know what that is? It's when everyone goes through all the junk they don't want. Then they put it outside their place for the Council to collect it. It only comes twice a year. It is the best thing that happens on our street. Lennie, my cousin who's twelve, has come over to go through my street's junk piles with me. Mum's given me her shopping trolley. It's on wheels and made of orange plastic. We can carry all the things we find back home to the garage.

Mum won't let me experiment in my room anymore. It's on account of the *incident*. It wasn't my fault. How could I have known? I just wanted to make some lights work.

I got some wire and attached it to two baby light bulbs and just put it on the prongs of an electric plug. It's when I stuck it into the electricity that *it* happened. A giant black explosion made all the lights in the house go off. And I got a bad electric shock. It hurt a lot. Mum said I was lucky I didn't have to go to hospital. It was lucky I wasn't dead. (Both Victoria and I lead dangerous lives.) Anyway now electricity is banned, except from batteries. And I have to do all my experiments in the garage.

You can't believe all the good stuff people throw out. The garbage trucks are coming next week to get it all, so we've got to work fast.

'Jamie and Lennie, the girls are going with you.'

'Oh Mum, no. They're stupid. They just want to find dolls and tea-sets and things, not proper stuff.'

7

'You don't go, if they don't go.'

'Let's stop mucking around,' Lennie calls out.

Lennie's the leader, mainly because he's the oldest and bossy and interesting. Lennie's smart. Smarter than me. He knows how to multiply everything properly and write stories fantastically, and he plays the cello. He's great at football and softball. Mum says I'm smart too. It's just that when Dad left us for his assistant, it made me stupid at school work. I don't understand why. I'm going to a doctor to fix it up, and to Auntie Lizzy (that's Lennie's and Roslyn's mum). Auntie Lizzy is a remedial teacher. She's giving me lessons to catch up.

I'm still smarter than Lennie at inventing. He admits that.

'Come here Jamie,' Lennie calls. He needs help. The thing's under a heap of junk. We sling things out of a giant cardboard box. There it is — a typewriter.

'It's broken Jamie. Leave it,' Lennie says.

'Are you kidding? This is the best. I can take it apart. There's stamps I can make out of the typewriting letters and ink ribbons. It's great.'

'All right then, Jamie. Put it in the trolley.'

Victoria runs up fast behind us. Lennie nearly steps on her. I shove her aside. Victoria isn't grateful. 'Don't, Jamie.' She tries to hit me. But I'm too quick for her. It sure is hard looking after her. Being Victoria's hero can be BORING.

Victoria gives Lennie a giant cuddle which makes him smile. 'Please can I put this green frog in the trolley?'

Can you believe it? The frog is stuffed and some of the stuffing is coming out of its leg. There's an eye missing too.

Lennie's a real sucker when it comes to Victoria. 'Not much room for the frog.' He looks at her. 'All right.' Maybe Lennie could marry Victoria when he's grown-up. Then we'd all be safe. Lennie and Roslyn's dad left them too.

When I'm a dad I'm never, ever going to leave my family. I'm going to be like Uncle Tom, that's my mum's brother. You know, he's like a regular dad. He's always at home and he goes on family holidays and he does barbeques and invites everyone over — Auntie Lizzy goes and Lennie and Roslyn and my mum and Victoria. I'm there too, of course. My Uncle Tom really loves his family. They're really happy. I'm going to be like that.

We've got heaps of stuff from the throw-out. We dump a load in the garage and go back for more. Lennie found part of a rock collection. He's a rock nut. He wants to be a geologist or a doctor or a builder. He can't decide. I think he'd make a great doctor because he loves cutting up things. You should have seen what he did to the octopus his mother bought for dinner. He took out the eyes first, then squashed the ink bag in it. Yuk. I'll never, ever be a doctor.

Mum should have been a doctor. She can fix up anything. When I get itchy bites, if there's no calamine lotion, Mum just presses the itchy bite and touches it in a special way and the itch goes. And with my stomach aches she's the best. Dad can't fix them.

My worst stomach aches are at night. That's sort of when I'm not a hero. That's when I'm ... I'll have to whisper again ... a coward.

Mum leaves the hall light on when I go to bed. It's not that I'm scared of the dark or anything. It's just so that Mum can see her way to the kitchen when she makes herself coffee. Mum makes a lot of coffee, except she never finishes her cup. She reckons it's because the phone rings or we kids want her or something. So after we go to sleep Mum drinks a whole cup of coffee.

Mum puts two pillows under my head — to stop my stomach ache — and she covers me with my favourite doona and she makes me put Chicky (my yellow chicken I was born with) next to me. She says she knows I don't need him because I'm older, but it makes her feel sad that he doesn't go to bed with me. Mum is having a lot of trouble accepting me growing up. I put Chicky next to me as a favour to her.

Then she tells me a story, to settle my stomach, she says. She makes me think of really nice things, like me lying on a warm sandy beach, or me floating on a soft fluffy white cloud. Mum's stuck shining stars and moons on the ceiling of my bedroom too, which protects me, so she says. It sort of makes my stomach ache better. But sometimes nothing works, and I get so scared. I don't even know what I'm scared of.

'Don't make too much of a mess in the garage,' Mum calls. She's got a tray with lots of apples and bananas cut up. 'You kids must be hungry.' She's bringing a giant bottle of diet lemonade as well. We're not allowed to have that on account of it belongs to Mum and it's not good for us. Mum's always on a diet. I wonder if it's because Dad used to call her fat. Mum's not fat. I've seen Dad's assistant — she's fat!

'A special treat since Lennie and Roslyn are here.'

'Thanks,' we all say. Then we eat while we investigate all the things we've collected.

Lennie and Roslyn are staying tonight because Auntie Lizzy is going out. I'm happy because Lennie will sleep on the top bunk in my room. I'm never as scared when Lennie sleeps with me.

'Come on, Victoria,' Roslyn says. 'Let's give the frog some apple and banana. We'll make a picnic for him.'

'Good, you're going to leave us alone,' I tell them. 'Come on Lennie, let's make a secret spy code from the typewriter letters.'

'All right super inventor,' Lennie laughs.

Jamie Discovers He's Not Alone

It's morning. Lennie's awake already. I had the best night. I dreamt about making an engine for my sailboat — the one I float in the bathtub. I've been planning it all night in my head. When I go to Dad's tonight he can help me make it.

Victoria and I stay with Dad one day every week, from six o'clock on Saturday night until six o'clock on Sunday night. Dad brings us home right on time because Mum gets mad otherwise.

I've got most of the parts to make the boat engine from the typewriter. It's lucky there's a throw-out. It's lucky Dad's so great at making things. Poor Mum isn't good at making inventions or being a handyman. She's only just learning to put in a light bulb. Luckily Auntie Lizzy's been divorced two years, so Auntie Lizzy's already learnt all that stuff that her husband used to do. She taught Mum how to put a light bulb in. Auntie Lizzy is showing Mum how to do lots of other things too — like mow the lawn and fix up my broken drawers. Auntie Lizzy says you should know those things even if there's a dad around.

I wish Dad would come home. I try my best to make him see how good I am when I stay with him. Victoria doesn't try very hard. Maybe Dad'll come back if we're really good. Then Mum can stop crying and we can be a happy family again, like Uncle Tom's.

Dad's assistant makes me sick. Guess what her name is? Belinda Chuck. Isn't that funny? Everyone calls her Belinda Chuck-it, even Mum. Auntie Lizzy, Lennie, Roslyn, Victoria, just everyone calls her that — except Dad. He wants us to like her. NEVER.

'Breakfast kids,' Mum calls out. The table is set with Victoria's Mickey Mouse bowl and plate set and three Peter Rabbit bowls and plates. There's a chip in one plate from when I knocked it over. Dad yelled at me a lot for doing that when he lived with us. But it was an accident. Mum told Dad to stop it. He used to yell at me all the time when he lived at home. He doesn't do it now. Dad shouted at Mum too when I broke the Peter Rabbit plate. He was so angry. I hate the chipped Peter Rabbit plate.

'Cornflakes or Weetbix?' Mum pours Cornflakes into the bowls. No one wants Weetbix. Then Victoria changes her mind. 'Mum I want Weetbix.' That was after Mum had poured the milk onto the Cornflakes. Usually Mum is soft and she'd change it for

Weetbix. But not this time. She says now that she's a single parent she's got to be tougher.

'Sorry Victoria. You get what you asked for first. We can't waste food.'

Victoria is so rude. 'That's not fair. You're mean Mum. I don't want it,' and she starts to cry. We all have to listen to Victoria crying while we eat our cereal, which gives me indigestion. Victoria's been like that ever since Dad left — a great big crier.

'Can we go to the park Mum?' I ask in between mouthfuls of cereal.

'Sure, after breakfast. I'll just get some drinks and chips for you kids. Four packets of chips should be right. That's to make sure you don't starve to death in the park.' Mum laughs this musical laugh and kisses the top of Lennie's head. She kisses Lennie because he's sitting right near her. Victoria straight away jumps out of her seat and forces Mum to kiss her as well, otherwise she'll have a tantrum.

Lennie's in charge of the food and drink supplies. 'Come on Roslyn, let's go.' Lennie's always bossing Roslyn around on account of her being younger, (she's ten like me), and on account of her being a wimp. Lennie can't stand wimps. He runs out of the door with me following him, then Victoria and lastly Roslyn. Roslyn runs slower than even Victoria.

We stop and look at some throw-out dumps on the way to the park. We're all carrying plastic bags to collect more stuff. The park is a really good one with two swings, one merry-go-round, monkey bars, a slippery dip and lots of grass to run around in. Victoria and Roslyn are on the monkey bars. Lennie and I grab the swings.

Lennie's brave. He swings so high he looks like he's flying. I'm trying to catch up to him because I'm brave too. The girls come around. They want the swings. 'OK OK,' and we get off. Lennie pushes Victoria for a while. 'That's enough Victoria,' and we go and lie on our stomachs in the grass. I start digging holes in the grass with a stick.

I take a big breath. I've been wanting to ask Lennie about this for a long, long time. 'Lennie, you know how your dad left you, when doesn't it feel rotten?'

'Oh. It gets better. Just takes a while.'

'Do you think your dad'll come back?'

'I used to think that he would.' Lennie looks at me seriously. 'Jamie, promise not to tell anyone?' I nod. Lennie waits a while before he starts talking again. 'I asked my dad if he'd come home and marry Mum again and be our proper father.' Lennie gets a stick and starts digging a hole in the grass as well. 'He said he was my dad and would always be my dad.' Lennie looks sad. 'But you know, he doesn't come to see me in my cello concerts, and he doesn't care what marks I get at school. He's never there when I'm in trouble. You know when I swallowed the needle, it was Mum who took me to the hospital and looked after me.'

'I remember that Lennie. It was a giant needle. I had to stay in the hospital with you and play Monopoly. My mum said it was so you wouldn't be bored and to keep you still. Actually, except for you swallowing the needle, the hospital was fun. I missed a day of school.' I watch Lennie.

Lennie hits the grass.

'Anyway Jamie, Dad isn't around.'

'Lennie, my dad's around. He always wants to see us. He's taking us camping next holidays.'

'Well, you're lucky Jamie.'

'Do you miss having your dad at home, Lennie?'

'Yes.'

'Me too. Lennie, I get scared inside sometimes.' I whisper, 'I get scared Mum's going to leave or even die, and who'll look after Victoria and me?'

'Sometimes, I used to get scared too. But, you know my mum will take care of you.' Lennie's hole in the grass is a giant one now.

'And my mum said she'd look after you and Roslyn if anything happened to Auntie Lizzy.'

I smile at my cousin Lennie. 'We're like twins, aren't we?'

'Yep Jamie, we're like twins.'

Jamie's Two Boats

Auntie Lizzy's collected Lennie and Roslyn already.
She's dropping them off at their dad's. They see their
dad at the same time Victoria and I see our dad. It
must be the law when mums and dads are divorced.

'Jamie, hurry up. Get the bits and pieces you want
your father to help you with. Your dad will be here
any minute.'

'Mum I'm doing it. You don't have to shout.'

'Stop being rude Jamie. I'm not shouting. Victoria
stand still. I can't do your hair if you keep moving
about.'

'Mummy, I'm not moving. I don't like the red
ribbon. I want pink.'

'I haven't got any more pink ribbons left. You
keep leaving them at your father's place. I'll buy you
some more but no more losing them. Good, your
hair's done.' Mum stares at Victoria. 'You look like a
princess.' Mum hugs Victoria.

'I love you Mummy,' Victoria says.

Dad's beeping the car horn outside. He's never

allowed inside the house again Mum says. I wish I could show him my room. Mum's put in new book shelves. Mum lets me take anything I want to Dad's house to show him. But I can't take him the book shelves can I?

'I love you kids. Have a nice time with your father. Jamie look after Victoria.'

I always do. I have to especially protect Victoria against Belinda Chuck-it. But it's so hard. Victoria is tricked into talking to her. I wish we could just see Dad by ourselves. Why does *she* have to be there?

Dad drives like a maniac Mum says. It's true, but I love it when he squeals around the corners. Victoria says to Dad to go faster, can you believe it?

'Dad can you help me make an engine for my toy boat? I've got all the parts.' I tell Dad about how Lennie and I found a typewriter in the throw-out and how we smashed it up and sorted the bits out. Dad's interested in everything, except it's hard to tell him about it because Victoria keeps interrupting about the green frog she found. It is *only* a stuffed toy. 'Keep quiet Victoria.'

'No, I want to tell Daddy.' She hits me. I can't escape because I'm sitting next to her in Dad's car — the ute, which is sort of like a truck. I hit her back.

'Stop it now, or you'll both get smacks from me,' Dad says, but he doesn't smack us. 'We're here anyway. Out of the car kids. I've got a surprise. It's in the garage.'

'What is it Daddy?' Victoria's holding Dad's hand and jumping up and down.

'You'll see.' Dad walks with big steps to the garage. My dad's more than six foot. He's tall. Mum said I'll be tall like him too. Do you know I'm nearly the tallest boy in my class?

Dad pushes up the garage door.

'Wow. It's the best.' I climb into it. 'A real boat Dad. I've always wanted a real boat. Can we go on it now?'

He laughs. 'Well, it is a bit late. We'll take it for a ride tomorrow. Is that OK?'

'Yes, yes. Dad I love you. You're the greatest Dad.' I hug Dad a lot and Victoria does too. We're so happy.

Dad's a very good cook. Nearly as good as Mum. We're having tomato soup. Dad only buys the best kind. It's from a red tin. He puts milk in the soup. Victoria's job is to stir it. I have to put the sausages under the grill. They're the thin kind of sausages — my favourite. Mum buys the fat sausages. We have corn and peas with them. Dad takes the peas out of the freezer.

It's good fun having dinner with Dad in his kitchen. Everything's right next to the table. You only have to lean your chair back to touch the sink or open the fridge. At home, with Mum you have to get up from the table if you want a glass or something from the cupboard.

But Dad's unit hasn't got a garden or anything. It's

on the main road too, so we can't go out by ourselves. It's different at home. We can ride our bikes on the footpath and put out the slip-and-slide on the grass. We turn the hose on fast, so that the slide is really wet and then ... wow, you should see me go on it — like a wet bullet. Victoria loves it too.

Dad opens the freezer. 'Who wants ice-cream?'

'Me, me,' Victoria shouts.

Victoria's noisy. Dad's bought chocolate chip ice-cream. Victoria digs out all the chocolate bits. She's a chocolate maniac. She'll do anything for chocolate. That's how I control her. I say, 'Victoria be nice and I'll give you chocolate. Victoria don't stand right in front of the TV and I'll give you chocolate. Victoria move over so I can sit down and I'll give you chocolate.'

'All right, where are those parts for your model boat engine Jamie?' Dad asks.

Dad is a genius making the engine. We work on the lounge room floor and he shows me how to put the wire together. Victoria sits right in his lap making a nuisance of herself. I have to put the engine on the boat. 'It's done Dad.'

Victoria's really smart for a six-year-old. She's been watching and knows straight away that we have to launch the model boat. Victoria and I know what each other's thinking a lot. It's on account of her being mine. Well, sort of. She was born because of me. I used to nag Mum all the time for a baby.

Nag, nag, nag. One day, she just said, 'All right. I'll give you a baby.' That was Victoria. It was funny when she was born. Guess what? When I looked inside her cot to see what type of baby Mum had given me, she was holding a chocolate bar. Mum said that Victoria came out of her tummy holding the chocolate because she knew what a special brother she had. Mum reckoned that Victoria heard me running around while she was inside her tummy and knew I'd look after her, as well as being a fun brother. I believed Mum then. That's because I was four. But now I know she was just playing a sort of trick on me, even though Victoria really was my present.

Victoria's filled the bathtub with cold water. She's not allowed to touch the hot water tap, ever since she nearly got burnt to death. As usual, I had to be a hero and save her.

Mum was in the kitchen cooking dinner and had the news turned on. She couldn't hear Victoria. Victoria was sitting in the bath and wanted more water and turned on the red tap instead of the blue one. I heard her screaming because she got so scared she couldn't think of what tap to turn off. I turned the HOT tap around and around and saved my sister. She wasn't burnt to death. Victoria and I do lead dangerous lives.

We're testing the sailboat. 'It's like a racing speedboat Dad,' I announce. 'It's so great. Thanks

Dad.' Dad rubs my hair and Victoria puts her hand into Dad's. I wish Mum was here. Why did Dad leave us? We miss him so much.

'The model boat's good, but tomorrow kids, we'll go out in the big boat. It should be a nice day.'

It's a Rotten Day

It's a rotten day. I was scared all night. I don't know what about. I kept dreaming I was drowning in the boat. I hate being a coward. Mum wasn't even there. She makes the dreams go away.

Now it's an even *worse* day. I wanted to go on the big boat so much. It's shiny aluminium with a black engine at the back and oars and enough room for six people. Wish there was only enough room for three people. Guess who's coming? Belinda Chuck-it. Revolting. Dad can see her any old time. Why doesn't he just want to be with us? We only have him for one day a week.

Belinda Chuck-it's standing in the kitchen helping Dad pack a picnic lunch. Victoria's buttering bread helping Belinda Chuck-it. My sister's truly stupid sometimes. She wants everyone to like her, even Belinda Chuck-it. Victoria's got worse since the divorce. She goes up to anyone and sits on their lap and holds their hands. I try to tell her it's dangerous. It worries me so much, because Mum says I've got to look after Victoria. How can I?

When Belinda Chuck-it comes into Dad's place she says hello to me. I say hello back, but I just walk away when she asks me anything else. Mum told me to be polite (because Dad'd be angry at me if I wasn't). So I am polite but I wouldn't want to talk to that person. She's — UGLY. She's got a giant nose and brown long curly hair and no chin. Dad can't you see how *ugly* she is? My mum is really pretty.

Belinda Chuck-it buys Victoria and me lots of presents and says nice things when Dad's there. I know it's her secret plan. She wants Dad to marry her. So she's got to make us like her. Dad wouldn't marry her if we hated her. I feel a stomach ache coming on. I haven't had one for ages.

'Come on Jamie, we're ready to leave,' Dad shouts. Dad's got this trailer which he pulls behind the ute.

Victoria's laughing. 'The boat's chasing us Daddy. You have to drive faster.'

'Victoria you're a speed maniac,' Dad says to her. She giggles and hugs me, which is cute after all the hitting she's been doing lately.

The water is light blue and calm. I love it. Dad drives the ute backwards down the ramp. We get out and push the boat off the trailer into the water.

I'm the captain. Dad lets me steer the boat. There's this handle that I have to turn that makes the boat go one way or the other. I nearly land on a sandbank, but my quick thinking saves us from a crash.

'Jamie steer towards the shore.' Dad puts his hand over mine, just to give me a little bit of help, but I know how to do it. 'Great job, Jamie.' We land on the sandy beach. Dad jumps over the side. 'Give me the anchor.' I drag the anchor from under the seat. It's heavy. I can see Dad thinks I'm very strong.

'Out of the way,' I say to Victoria.

'I'm not in the way,' Victoria announces, then helps carry the rope tied to the anchor. She's useful sometimes. We're like a team.

Belinda Chuck-it's given up talking to me. Good. Now she's lying on the beach sunbaking *without blockout*. Maybe she'll turn into a red lobster. Dad's talking to her. How boring. Victoria and I get our buckets. We're going shell collecting. Maybe I'll find some interesing rocks for Lennie's rock collection too.

'Jamie look what I've found!' Victoria shows me this stupid oyster shell. As if that's special!

'Great,' I say. I should tell her oyster shells are nothing, but Mum's not here and Dad's talking to Belinda Chuck-it, so it's ME who's got to look after her. I grab Victoria's hand and find a very interesting rock pool. We bend down and I show her some crabs and soft green seagrass and shells that move. We pick up some shells which are silver, but in the sunlight look like rainbows. I find a smooth white speckled rock. I'll keep it for Lennie. Victoria picks up a giant white shell which looks like a snail's house. But I find the greatest thing — it's got to be a shark's tooth. It's white and pointy. Victoria's a quick learner. She throws away the oyster shell, without me even telling her.

The boat trip back is excellent. Belinda Chuck-it is *red*. She can't move much. Every time the boat jumps over a wave she crunches up her face. It's because her back hurts.

Mum never told me Belinda Chuck-it was stupid. She couldn't look after us. Mum always makes us wear T-shirts when we're at the beach. We're not allowed to die of skin cancer. Dad drops Belinda Chuck-it off at her place. She can hardly walk. I start laughing.

'What are you laughing about?' Dad asks suspiciously.

'Nothing, Dad. It was a great day, that's all.' We hug Dad a lot when he drops us back home.

Stomach Aches Can Get Better

It's Monday afternoon. That's the day Auntie Lizzy teaches me writing. I hear Lennie and Roslyn and Victoria playing in the backyard on Lennie's trampoline. Why can't I be there? It's not fair.

'Pay attention Jamie,' Auntie Lizzy says. She's very strict when she's teaching me. I've heard Mum and Auntie Lizzy talk about me. They worry that I won't catch up. That I'll be stupid. Then they talk about Dad. This gives me stomach aches.

'Your work is improving, Jamie. That's the first time you've written a whole story.'

I smile. Maybe I *can* catch up.

'You have to do this writing and reading for the next lesson.'

'That's a lot of work,' I say, looking at two pages of exercises she's given me. Yuk.

'I want it done.' Auntie Lizzy has a serious look in her eyes. I suppose I'll have to do it. Mum says she and Auntie Lizzy are only making me have lessons because they love me.

Mum keeps telling me, 'How can you be an inventor if you can't read and write?' Doesn't Mum understand? I'm an inventor NOW, ALREADY, TODAY.

We're having dinner at Auntie Lizzy's. We do that a lot these days. Mum used to make these fantastic baked dinners with roast lamb or chicken and potatoes and peas and cauliflower. I never ate the cauliflower.

Mum'd serve up everything. But Dad'd shout, 'Where's the cream sauce for the cauliflower?' Mum hadn't made any sauce. Then Mum'd go red and nearly cry. I think that's one of the reasons Dad left. I don't understand why? I hate cauliflower. And I hate cream sauce even more.

I don't like Auntie Lizzy's cooking much. She makes spinach pies and vegetables on rice, and soups made out of stuff I don't recognise. I cross my fingers.

'Delicious,' says my mum.

Oh, no. It's the dreaded spinach pie. Everyone eats. I'm starving *and* I'm a growing boy! At least there's a fruit platter after. I grab some apples and pears. That'll have to do until I get home and raid the fridge. I think Mum bought my favourite cheese, and oh yeh, there's chocolate milk and passionfruit.

'Mum, when are we going home?' I ask.

'Soon, Jamie. You're not usually in a hurry to

leave.' Mum looks at Roslyn and Lennie. 'Don't you want to play with your cousins for a little while?'

'Maybe.' My stomach really hurts. It's starvation. I learnt at school that there's acid juices in your stomach which squash up the food so your body can use it. If there's no food, the acid juices just squash up your stomach I think. My stomach's squashed.

Mum and Auntie Lizzy are talking to each other and drinking coffee. They always talk about the same things — why the dads left, and us. Except Auntie Lizzy is talking about a man she's going out with. He takes Lennie and Roslyn swimming like a real dad. He even takes me and Victoria too. I like him. Maybe Auntie Lizzy will get married again.

'Come on Jamie.' I follow Lennie and Roslyn and Victoria up to Lennie's room. Lennie's got gold football statues on his shelf. He's terrific at sport and there's awards for being clever at school. When will I be clever?

Victoria's sitting on Lennie's lap. Roslyn's eating some jelly snakes. My favourite kinds are the red and orange snakes. Don't like the green ones much.

'Can I have a red one, Roslyn?' She sees the starving look on my face and feels sorry for me. She's being kind today and gives everyone two snakes. Sometimes she won't give anyone anything. It's on account of her being beautiful. Everyone tells her that and gives her things because she's beautiful. Wish I was — not beautiful, but handsome.

Roslyn's got thick curly light-brown hair, green eyes and big white teeth. I can see bits of yellow snake stuck in them. Sometimes it goes to her head, being beautiful. Then she's a bit mean. But inside, Roslyn's kind.

I'm not starving now, but I still have a stomach ache. It feels like a knife is stuck in it.

'Your turn Jamie. Throw the dice. What's wrong with you?'

Lennie must have seen the pained look on my face. It's hard playing Ludo when you feel like me. I throw the dice. 'Just a stomach ache.'

Lennie nods. 'Your turn Roslyn.' Lennie pokes Roslyn in the stomach.

'Don't do that. It hurts,' Roslyn whinges.

She's done it now. It's the whine in her voice. I look at Roslyn sadly because I know Lennie's going to hit her.

He does. A BIG ONE.

'Just have your go Roslyn.'

Roslyn's crying. 'I'm going to tell Mum.'

'Go on. We won't play then. Just run off and cry to Mum. Roslyn you're stupid.' Lennie has a bad temper. He chucks Victoria off his lap and throws himself on his bed.

'I'm not stupid,' Roslyn whinges, 'and I'm telling.'

'Shut up Roslyn.'

It's the end. Roslyn runs out of the room crying to

tell her mum. I must be still looking pained. Or maybe Lennie feels better after shouting at Roslyn. Lennie calls out. 'Come here, on the bed.' He looks at my stomach. 'Lie on your back Jamie. You know, I saw a doctor do this in a movie. Lift up your shirt.'

I pull up my shirt. Lennie starts rubbing my stomach softly. My stomach ache feels the same.

'Roslyn had lots of stomach aches when our dad left. Maybe it's the same thing, Jamie.'

This is an interesting thought. 'Will the stomach aches go away?'

'Yes. Roslyn's did. She doesn't have them much anymore.' Lennie looks at me seriously, but still keeps rubbing my stomach. 'You know, it's great having just a mum, all to yourselves. Jamie, your mum is the best, like mine.'

I nod.

'Jamie, we're lucky.'

Guess what? Lennie's fingers are working. Really working — my stomach ache's going.

The Beginning of a Special Experiment

My dad says that Mum's weak, soft, gives in. He's right. Luckily, that's good for me. I'm making the best, most interesting, most secret invention — *in my room.*

I thought Mum would never let me invent anything in my room again, after the electricity experiment. But all I had to do was bother and bother her. She's too tired to say anything but yes, after teaching at school. I suppose it's a bit mean of me to bother her then. But my inventions are really important. I just have to do them. And the garage is too dark at night to work in. I can't leave Mum and Victoria alone in the house then, can I?

I still use the garage, mainly on weekends — it's got more space than my bedroom. But it's really true, that at night Mum needs me in the house so she's not alone. And also, in case she has to hang a poster or fix a cupboard or something. Mum's still not as good as Auntie Lizzy at handy jobs. I think she'll never be much good at it. So it's pretty terrific that I'm an expert at being a handyman, and an inventor.

Victoria is my assistant. She's helping me invent. Victoria hands me the screwdriver and different tools when I need them. She also does useful things, like holding the wood still while I hammer a nail into it, and getting me a drink of orange cordial. Sometimes she spills the drink, but she's getting better. Mum gets mad when she splashes it on the carpet. 'Orange never comes out,' Mum says annoyed. Then Mum runs to get a sponge to mop it up.

So far I've attached some batteries to wire. 'Glue, Victoria.' I need it to stick the paddle-pop sticks together. That's for the casing around the batteries. Lennie and Roslyn have been saving paddle-pop sticks for me, as well as Victoria and me saving our paddle-pop sticks. I've got a bucket full of them. They're a big part of my invention.

Mum's stuck her head around the door. 'Bedtime, kids.' I open my mouth, just to say I need a little bit more time. But Mum is really unreasonable at bedtime (not like Dad). She says, 'Don't bother asking'. I think Mum can read my mind. 'Brush your teeth NOW.' This is the main thing Mum is strict about. She says we can't cope with school if we're tired. Dad doesn't think it's important. He lets us stay up till midnight if we want. I told Mum that.

She just said, 'It's all right on the weekends, but not on school days. I have to worry about your

education.' I wish Mum wouldn't worry about it. I'd rather stay up LATE. 'I've bought you bubble-gum flavoured toothpaste, kids.'

'Thanks Mum, you're the best.' While I'm saying this, Victoria's already running into the bathroom.

'I'm brushing first,' Victoria screams out speeding past me.

'You're so greedy,' I scream back at her. Victoria's left toothpaste all over the basin. She's disgusting. 'Can't you brush your teeth without a mess?'

'Be quiet, Jamie,' she says with toothpaste dripping from her mouth. Victoria is definitely disgusting.

'You kids stop fighting and hurry up.' Mum's standing watching us.

'Come on,' she calls.

Mum tucks Victoria into bed first, because Mum knows I need her at bedtime. Bedtime's when I'm a little bit of ... a coward. Mum cuddles me and tells me I'm safe and makes me think of other things, like my invention.

'You're clever Jamie making things. What are you inventing now?'

'Don't know yet, Mum.'

'Then that's what you have to dream about tonight. What you're going to do with the paddle-pop sticks and the batteries.'

I try to think about my inventing because I want to be brave, not afraid. But it's scary in the dark.

Vince is a Bully

I hate school. I can't think in class. The teacher, Mrs Birtwhistle, shouts all the time. It's on account of Vince. Vince is BIG with muscles everywhere, including in his brains if you ask me. Maybe that's why he can't do anything else except bash up kids. Twice he broke his arm doing that. His arm's not broken now though. He hangs around the toilets waiting. I just can't hold on all day. I have to go. My friend Joshua and I have a plan. Joshua is going to run in front of him and distract Vince, while I speed in. Here goes.

He's calling out. 'Vince, those guys want you. Come on.'

My friend starts running. Vince follows. My friend's going to disappear behind the Art Room in a minute. Vince's gone. I dash into the toilets. RELIEF. Ahhhh. But I hate school, even without Vince there. Mrs Birtwhistle talks and talks, but I can't understand her. We're doing multiplication tables and in the middle she's shouting at some kids and I can't hear her. Other kids hear her. They know their tables. Not me. I'm STUPID. I feel sick.

'Excuse me Miss,' I call out. You have to call out in her class. It's so noisy.

'Yes, Jamie.'

'I'm going to vomit.'

'Leave the classroom. Wash your face.' Mrs Birtwhistle turns away from me because Vince is tearing a poster off the wall. 'Stop that Vince.' Mrs Birtwhistle's red in the face. She doesn't care if I vomit. I want to go home.

Today's the day I get my half-yearly school report, too. Sick and a report. Pretty bad combination, don't you think?

The school bell goes. Victoria waits for me outside her classroom. She's in first class. The kids are so cute in first class. They all know I'm Victoria's big brother and I'm in fifth class. I've told Victoria, 'If anyone bothers you tell them that your big brother will get them.' The first class kids wouldn't dare tease Victoria.

'Victoria, where's your hat? Put it on.' It's the school rule that everyone has to wear a hat so that you don't get sunburnt. You get into heaps of trouble for not wearing it. In any case, Mum is a nut about us wearing hats. Victoria is such a responsibility.

'No. I'm not doing what you say.' Victoria's in one of *those* moods.

'OK, I'm walking home *without* you.' She hates me doing that. I run really fast.

'Stop it Jamie.' She's running after me puffing.

'Put your hat on.'

'OK, Jamie.'

There's a playground on the way home. We always stop for a swing. I push Victoria. She loves it. Mum'll be driving into the driveway when we get home. Maybe she'll forget that I get my report today. Please forget, Mum. We're home. Mum sees us.

'Hi, kids. Help me unload the car and then I'll get you something to eat. Are you hungry?'

'Mum, I'm so tired.' Victoria puts on this exhausted look. It's not the truth. At the park she was running around like a maniac. She just doesn't want to help get the things out of the car. I bet Mum'll let her off. Dad's right. Mum's too soft.

'You do look tired, princess.'

'What a load of garbage!' I say under my breath.

'Go inside Victoria, and I'll make you your favourite tomato and cheese sandwich in a minute.'

I help Mum. I have to, given the report problem.

'You're such a good boy, Jamie.' Mum kisses me. She looks white and has bags under her eyes.

We unpack the shopping together in the kitchen, and I tell Mum about Vince.

'I'm going to see the Headmistress about him. It's not good enough.'

'Don't, Mum. Vince'll know and then it'll be worse. And Mrs Birtwhistle'll be angry.'

'Jamie, I promise to fix it up. It'll be better for you.'

I want to argue with Mum, except she's looking at me seriously. I know she's going to ask me. She does.

'Where's your report, Jamie?'

I drag it out of my school bag. Mum's reading it slowly. She finishes, stares at me, touches my hand. 'Is the work too hard, Jamie?'

The report must be rotten. I shake my head and whisper. 'No, Mum.'

'Jamie, can't you concentrate in class?'

'It's so noisy, and I can't think when the teacher's talking, and I don't know. Do I have to go to school?'

'Yes, you have to go to school. You want to be a grown-up inventor one day, don't you?' Mum puts her arms around me. 'It's hard when mums and dads divorce. It makes kids sad, confused. Then it's too difficult to listen to the teacher sometimes.'

When Mum says that I get this funny feeling right in my stomach.

'And Jamie, it looks like your teacher needs to know you a lot better. You're smart, Jamie. You're my clever boy.'

Mum hugs me a lot. I don't know why, but I feel better.

Mrs Birtwhistle Likes Mum

Mum's made an appointment with the Headmistress, but she's seeing my teacher, Mrs Birtwhistle, first.

'Jamie, you mind Victoria while I talk to your teacher,' Mum says.

I don't want to. What's Mum going to say to my teacher? Why can't I listen? I feel a big pain in my stomach. I beg Mum, 'Can't I stay?'

'I want to stay, too,' Victoria whinges.

'Be quiet, Victoria.' I pinch her.

Victoria screams. 'Jamie hurt me.' She's crying really loudly and Mum's going red.

'Stop the fighting. I can't cope with this. JUST STOP IT.' Mum doesn't usually get so upset when we fight. Well, not straight away. But she looks like she's going to cry. Mrs Birtwhistle comes out of the classroom.

'Please kids.' Mum wipes her face with her hand and takes a giant breath. 'Please, don't make this fuss.'

I feel lousy. I don't want Mum to cry. Victoria holds onto Mum's dress. Victoria gets to go into the classroom with Mum and my teacher. I have to stand outside the door. I'm going to try and listen to EVERYTHING they say. Well, it is about *me*.

'Jamie's finding it difficult to concentrate in class and he's not working well,' Mrs Birtwhistle tells Mum.

'My Jamie's bright, Mrs Birtwhistle.'

I love my mum.

'Well, I don't know, but he's not performing,' Mrs Birtwhistle says.

'He's had a lot to put up with, since his father and I got divorced.' Mum gets really quiet. I can hardly hear her.

'My ex-husband and I are hostile.' I wonder what that means. 'You know, he left with his assistant?' Mum laughs. That's not funny. I hate Belinda Chuck-it. And, Dad forces us to be polite to her. She's living with our dad I think. We never, ever get to see him by ourselves anymore.

My stomach ache's getting bad. I can't stand it. Mum and Mrs Birtwhistle are still talking. I'm too sick to make out what they're saying. Mum I need you.

I stick my head inside the classroom. Mrs Birtwhistle see me. 'We're finished Jamie, you can come in.'

Thank goodness.

'You've got a nice mother, Jamie,' Mrs Birtwhistle says.

Everyone knows that. Everyone knows I have the BEST mum.

I whisper to Mum, 'I feel sick.'

'It's all right, Jamie, we're going home soon.' Mum rubs my stomach. 'I just have to have a few words to the Headmistress about Vince.'

'Mum, I want to go home.'

Mum keeps walking. 'I have to see the Headmistress. My appointment's soon. I'll be quick.'

Victoria and I wait for ages and ages outside the school office. The Headmistress' door is shut and I can't hear a thing. Mum comes out. It looks like she's been crying. She kisses us. 'I love you kids.'

Mum's quiet in the car. I keep telling her I'm sick and Victoria keeps saying she's hungry. I dig into my pockets. I remember stuffing a few chocolate Smarties in my shorts yesterday. Found them. I give her the chocolate. Victoria stops complaining.

When we get home, Mum just gets out of the car without saying *one* word. We follow her inside the house. She makes dinner. We eat, then have a bath. Mum reads us a story.

It's so quiet. 'Mum, my stomach hurts.'

'I know Jamie.' She strokes my stomach and the pains feel a bit better.

'Your teacher is going to sit you at the front of the room so you can hear everything. The Headmistress said Vince is leaving next term. So he won't be at the school that much longer. Things should be better.'

Mum stands up from the bed. That's where she's been sitting. 'Have beautiful dreams. Be happy.'

'I can't Mum.'

Mum stops. 'You know, you can make yourself happy. I wish I could make you happy and stop your stomach aches, but I can't. Only you can, Jamie.'

'I can't.'

Victoria is a copy-cat. 'Jamie can't, Mummy.'

'Just remember, you're brave and strong. Even if grown-ups do stupid things, like getting a divorce, you don't have to be sad and sick. Just say to yourself *Jamie is happy* and you'll be happy.'

'It's hard Mum.'

'Yes, it's hard. But I'll be here for you, always. I'll never leave you. Your dad loves you too, in his own way. Auntie Lizzy loves you too, and Lennie and Roslyn and Uncle Tom. Both of you kids are safe. Really safe.'

'Mum, what's hostile mean.'

Mum stops to think. Then says, 'It's when people are angry at each other. When mums and dads divorce, a lot of the time they're angry at each other. But they're *never* angry at the kids. Your dad and I aren't angry at you.' Mum says softly, 'Go to sleep now. I know your dreams are going to be wonderful tonight. Dream of inventing new things Jamie.'

'What can I dream about?' Victoria pipes in.

'Ice-cream cake and birthday parties, Victoria.' Mum laughs and grabs my sister's hand to take her to Victoria's bedroom.

I like Mum laughing.

'Mum, I'm still working on something. I can't think of another invention before I'm finished.'

'All right, dream about what you're going to do next with it. Enough already. It's late. So, goodnight. Sleep tight. Don't let the bedbugs bite.'

'Leave the hall light on Mum,' I call out.

'I always do Jamie.'

Frogs are Green

Mrs Birtwhistle is nicer since Mum's talk. She keeps smiling at me, now that I'm sitting in the front row. Vince is right at the back of the classroom. I think he's hitting the boy in front of him. Vince isn't interested in me anymore. Great. I'm concentrating on Mrs Birtwhistle's lesson about drawing a map of the world. I love map drawing. Mum gave me an atlas. Can you believe that it was her school atlas? It's very old. And, my mum must have been a bit bad at school, because I've found notes she's written in it to her friend.

'The teacher's got stinky breath. I hope she doesn't come near me.' Mum wrote that.

Mum's friend's scribbled back. 'She coughed at me already. Horrible.'

'I bet she never washes. Ha! Ha!' That's my mum's answer.

Right next to the map of France, Mum's written, 'Frogs are green and jumpy'. I think that means that the French are frogs on account of them eating frogs' legs. My cousin Lennie told me about that once. Maybe all the frogs in France are on crutches. I start laughing. Mrs Birtwhistle stares at me. I laugh louder. I don't want to. I can't help it.

'Jamie stop that laughing.' I can't.

'Sorry, but it's on account ... of ... (ha, ha, ha) ... the ... frogs ... on crutches.'

'Frogs? Crutches? Jamie stop that laughing.' I'm hysterical by now. 'Right, Jamie. Go and stand outside the Headmistress' Office.'

Mrs Birtwhistle is angry. If you ask me, it's not my fault that the whole class started making croaking noises. Vince comes out with the biggest croak I've ever heard.

'Jamie, you just stay outside the office until the lunch bell.'

'It's unfair, Miss,' I try to explain. Mrs Birtwhistle doesn't listen.

'Just GO,' she screams.

Vince is jumping around at the back on arms and legs like a frog. Why doesn't Mrs Birthwhistle send him to stand outside the Headmistress' Office? Why me? I'm not laughing anymore.

There's only ten minutes till the bell rings. I keep praying that the Headmistress won't come out of her office. My shoes are filthy. I rub one shoe against the back of my leg. Then the other. I'm wearing a black tracksuit so no one'll see the rub marks. Five minutes to go. Sweat is starting to run down my face. Maybe the Headmistress will think I've got a temperature and that's why I'm standing here. Three minutes. I hear the phone ring from inside the office. It stops ringing. Two minutes. The Headmistress is talking on the phone. One minute.

'Sixty, fifty-nine, fifty-eight, fifty-seven ... forty, forty-one ... thirty-one... twenty ... nine, eight, seven ... three, two, one.' The bell. I run into the playground, just in time to see the Headmistress' door open. Saved.

Mum's going to be mad at me if she finds out. Hope Mrs Birtwhistle forgets. She forgets most other things, except for Vince.

School will never, ever get better.

Mum's home when Victoria and I open the front door. She's on the phone talking to Auntie Lizzy. I don't want her to be talking to Auntie Lizzy.

'Hi, kids. Change your school clothes. There's fruit and biscuits on the table,' Mum calls out, then she starts talking to Auntie Lizzy again, but in a whisper. I hate that. It's probably about me and how hopeless I'm at school. I've got to go to my special lesson with Auntie Lizzy tomorrow *and* I haven't done the work she said I had to do.

Luckily Victoria bangs her head on the cupboard drawer while she's pulling out her favourite pink top from the drawer. She's crying loudly. *Very* loudly.

'Sorry Lizzy, I have to go. Victoria's hurt herself.' Mum puts down the phone.

Sometimes Victoria is VERY useful.

Mum comes back into the kitchen holding Victoria's

hand. She sits at the table. Victoria gets onto Mum's lap. I'm too big for that. Mum tells us about the naughty kids she teaches and we laugh and laugh and eat apples and peaches in between.

'Mum, why are frogs green and jumpy?'

Mum looks at me oddly. 'Frogs? What are you talking about?'

'It's in your old school atlas. You wrote that next to France.' I run and get Mum the atlas.

'I can't believe it. I did write that. Maybe I was twelve. Why did I do it?' Mum thinks. Then giggles. 'Oh, yes. We had to do a project on France. I was doing food. The French eat funny things Jamie — snails and goose's liver and the legs of poor little frogs. Do you want frogs' legs for dinner tonight?'

'No!' Victoria shouts.

'Maybe we'll have chicken instead. What do you think?'

'Chicken,' Victoria and I say together.

We clear up the dishes. Victoria only carries her cup to the sink. But I've got to help Mum the most. Mum says, 'Jamie, you're my big helper.' I sort of like that.

Victoria goes to do some drawings. She's making cards for Mum and me. Mum goes to her desk. She's marking English essays for school, and I've got a brilliant idea. The frogs have given me a genius thought for my invention.

This invention is going to be the best.

Jamie's Invention is a Secret

Victoria's on guard. I don't want anyone, not even Mum, to see this.

'Jamie, no one's coming into the room. PLEASE can I help?'

'NO, just stand on guard.'

Victoria starts moaning. 'I don't want to.'

I decide to take pity on her. This is mainly since she will probably cry and tell Mum that I'm mean. I'm never, ever mean.

'Put my chair against the door. Then if anyone comes in, the chair'll move and we can stop them getting inside.'

Victoria drags my chair across the room and nearly squashes a battery. 'Stop it, you idiot. Can't you watch out?' You can see, I DO have a lot to put up with, with Victoria.

'I'm not an idiot. If you say I'm an idiot, I'm going.'

Mum shouts out from her desk. She's still marking schoolwork. 'You kids stop fighting.'

'We're not Mum,' I call back. I was going to tell Mum that Victoria is a pest and nearly wrecked my battery. But I am supposed to mind her, and anyway, I need her to hold the paddle-pop sticks.

'Don't move.' Victoria's not too bad. She holds the sticks *very* still while I glue them onto a wood base. Victoria is a good assistant. I stick a wire onto the battery.

'It's working. It's working,' I scream out to Victoria.

She sticks her finger into the middle of my invention.

'It's very good, Jamie.'

I nod. 'All we need now is a frog.'

I hide my invention under my double bunk, then grab Victoria by her dress. That's mainly to get her to move quickly. 'Come on. You're so slow.'

'I am not, Jamie. And you're wrecking my dress.'

I pull her behind me all the way to Mum's desk. 'Can we go to Lennie's and Roslyn's house?'

Mum looks at her watch.

'There's lots of time before dinner Mum. I'll set the table now. Please, it's *very* important.'

'Well, I've still got a bit of marking to do. All right, but ring Auntie Lizzy first. If she says it's all right, then you can go.'

'Thanks, thanks, you're the nicest mum.' Mum laughs and hugs me. I like that.

'Where's my hug, Mummy? It's not fair, you always hug Jamie.' Victoria complains as loudly as she can, so Mum hugs her hard, which is really kind. I'd give Victoria a hit on the head if I was Mum. She's really, truly an idiot of a sister sometimes.

I run nearly all the way to Lennie's and Roslyn's house with Victoria whingeing the whole time about me going too fast. Lennie's out the front of his house throwing a basketball into a ring and Roslyn's watching. That's because Lennie won't let her play. She looks miserable. Uncle Tom hammered the basketball ring up for Lennie.

My Uncle Tom is special.

'Lennie, Lennie, I need your ...' I'm puffing loudly, and can't say it at first. Victoria's puffing too.

Roslyn calls out, 'Victoria! Great, I'm sick of watching Lennie and his dumb basketball. Do you want to play with me?'

The girls go off to Roslyn's bedroom. I get my breath back. 'Lennie, I need ... Herman.'

'Herman? Why?'

'Herman's important for my invention. I really need him.' Lennie should be understanding, especially since he's gone off Herman lately. It's on account of Sarah. He likes her better.

'Maybe. I'll see how Herman feels about it.'

We go into Lennie's bedroom quietly. Herman's asleep. He looks cute with his bulging eyes and lime green legs. 'Mum wants to eat Herman's legs,' I tell

Lennie laughing. Just then, Victoria comes into Lennie's room.

'Mum does not,' she yells out.

Victoria can't take a joke — and she wakes up Herman. Herman's jumping around in his cage on account of the shock. Victoria can give the loudest yells you can imagine.

'Be quiet, Victoria. You're an idiot.'

Victoria pinches me and then runs out of the room as fast as she can. I've got more important things to do than chase her. My arm's sore. She has a strong pinch.

Herman's got a great cage — pretty big, with a pond for him to splash in and plants and rocks of course. Lennie's rock collection is enormous. But I think he's only lending Herman a few of the big rocks.

'Only kidding about the legs, Lennie.'

'I'm not dumb, Jamie. I know.' Lennie looks seriously at Herman.

'I'd eat your legs, if you ate Herman's.'

I don't bother answering that. I've got to get Lennie to give me Herman.

'Herman's just what I need. I'll look after him. I'll put water in the pond. Please can I borrow him, just for a little while? Please. And you do have Sarah now.' Sarah's a big, white rat.

A bit of bargaining goes on here. Lennie's pretty tough. He wants me to lend him my roller-blades for *a week* and I love my roller-blades. He also wants me to give him my second favourite piece of white quartz. (I'm starting a rock collection too.) Lennie's not brave enough to ask for my favourite piece.

'It's a deal. Can I have Herman now? I'll give you the roller-blades and the rock on Monday.' I get this sincere look on my face. Lennie must know I can be trusted.

'All right.'

Auntie Lizzy drives me and Victoria home, on account of it being too difficult to carry Herman in his cage, all the way back to my house. Lennie and Roslyn come for the drive.

My mum asks everyone to stay for dinner. 'We've got lots of honey chicken wings,' she tells Lennie. Mum makes the best honey chicken wings in the world. They're Lennie's favourite. My dad always used to say he hated them. He says Mum is a bad cook. That's not true. Mum's chicken wings are fantastic.

Everyone's talking about chicken wings. 'I'm starving,' Lennie tells my mum. 'I'm starving,' Victoria copies. 'I'm starving,' Roslyn says so too. Everyone runs to the table for dinner. It's funny.

No one notices me put Herman in my bedroom.

Dad's on Saturday

Herman croaked *all night*.

I'm exhausted. I don't know how Lennie does it. I wouldn't live with Herman for anything. Anyway I won't have to sleep with him tomorrow night. It's Saturday. You already know that Victoria and I stay with Dad on Saturday night.

I can't wait to tell Dad about Herman, except *she'll* probably be there. Belinda Chuck-it. Dad'll want to talk to her and then she'll pretend she cares about my inventions.

I heard her tell someone on the phone that she's not interested in science, or inventions. It's true — she doesn't like science. She probably hates it. You should have heard her scream when she found my raw chicken bones. I'd put them in a bottle with holes in the lid and buried them. It's just that I'd dug up the bottle a bit early. It was very interesting. Belinda Chuck-it said the chicken bones were alive. It was *only* the bugs and things. She's dumb. How else can I make fossils?

Belinda Chuck-it spoils everything.

I've just got a brilliant idea for Saturday night.

Dad's beeping his car horn to get us. He just traded-in his ute for a super-great four-wheel drive for camping. Mum only has the old station wagon. At least it's red. But Dad's car is silver with dark grey stripes along the sides and it's got bull bars and giant wheels. I love his car. Wish Mum could have a go in it. I get a stomache ache when I think about Mum never, ever having a ride in Dad's super-great car.

'Hurry up,' Dad calls out. Victoria helps me with my brilliant idea. It's pretty dark. So we carry it slowly to Dad's four-wheel drive. Belinda Chuck-it is sitting in the front.

'What have you there, Jamie?' she asks. She smiles at Dad so that he can see how interested she is in me. She's not. It's sickening.

'You'll like it,' I tell her. 'Put your hand through there.' Belinda Chuck-it sticks her hand in, all the time smiling and looking at Dad.

Dad nearly smashes into another car. It's on account of the screaming. Belinda Chuck-it screams and screams. Poor Victoria starts crying because of the noise. I put my arm around her, even though I'm getting a headache. Victoria snuggles into my arms. She's cute. But that Belinda Chuck-it isn't cute — she's nuts. I thought it'd make her sort of, surprised. A normal person would have given one yell or shout and then laughed. But Belinda Chuck-it is amazing.

She's still screaming. You'd think she'd never touched anything green and a little bit slimy. Poor Herman, maybe it wasn't such a brilliant idea.

I should have left Herman at home. Mum's good at looking after my live things. She'd feed Herman and not care that he's slimy. She looks after my budgies and the cat. But she hates cleaning the walking-fish tank. It's on account of the green fungus. Mum says I should clean the tank, but the tank's too heavy for me to move. You have to put my walking-fish in a bowl with water and tip out the water from the tank. Then you have to scrub the fungus off before filling up the tank. Anyway, Mum's done it so many times she's an expert. I think she really likes doing it now.

Uncle Tom gave us the walking-fish. He told Mum that we needed more males at home, so gave up two boy walking-fish. The big fat white one had four floppy legs sticking out of it. The thinner black one had short strong legs. You should see the black one move in the tank. Fast.

'Mum, Mum,' I screamed one day. 'Look at the walking-fish.' There were hundreds and hundreds of little black things in the water. It looked like a bug attack.

Mum stared for a while. She started nodding her head back and forward with an amazed look on her face. 'That's just like Uncle Tom.' Mum looked at me. 'I think the white walking-fish is a girl.'

Victoria stuck her nose against the tank and had a very good look. 'There are lots of baby walking-fish.'

Only five days later the tank just had two walking-fish — the black one and the white one. Mum said it was disgusting. Mum said that she hates the walking-fish. It's only because she's not a scientist. She doesn't understand their survival instincts. They had to eat the baby walking-fish. Otherwise there wouldn't be enough room for them in the tank. They'd all die. But you know, they could have left one or two babies. Actually, I've gone off the walking-fish a bit ever since.

Herman's shaking. I suppose Victoria and I'll have to sleep with Herman to calm him down. Hope he doesn't croak too loudly again. I try to explain to Dad that Herman's part of my experiment and that I didn't want to make Belinda Chuck-it scream. No one would. It is a horrible noise. I cross my fingers when I tell Dad, on account of it being only half true. I wouldn't want to lie to Dad, even though Dad is ... (I hate to say this) ... a bit of a liar. I usually test Dad to see if he's telling the truth.

I ask him questions. 'Dad, why did you leave us?' 'I didn't leave you.' A LIE. 'Dad, why did Belinda Chuck-it make you go away?' 'She didn't have anything to do with it.' A LIE. 'Dad, why do you make Mum cry?' 'She makes herself cry.' A LIE. 'Dad do you love us?' 'Yes, I love both you kids.' THE TRUTH. Dad kisses us then.

I love my dad lots and lots and lots. Nearly as much as I love Mum. But I'd never lie to my mum, even with my fingers crossed. Dad forgives me about Herman. Belinda Chuck-it pretends to.

Herman
and Roller-blades

Herman is having a bad weekend. He's croaking all the time. He looks greener than usual. Victoria notices that. She's right. At last, Sunday six pm arrives. We can go home. Mum'll have to fix Herman because Lennie'll kill me if Herman dies. I still think Belinda Chuck-it's screaming did it, or Herman could have swallowed Lennie's rock. I can't find it in Herman's cage. But worst of all, if Herman dies, I can't get my invention to work.

We're really careful carrying Herman's cage (with Herman in it), to our front door.

'Mum, Mum,' I scream out.

'Mum, Mum,' Victoria screams out.

Mum opens the door. She knows straight away there's a problem. Mum's like that. 'Is Herman all right?' We shake our heads. 'He looks very green,' Mum says. Mum takes the cage and puts it in a quiet corner of the lounge room. She pours some water into

Herman's pond. 'Let's leave him alone. Herman's just exhausted. Don't scream around him. He'll be fine tomorrow.' Relief. Herman should be all right.

Mum smiles. 'Nice to have you kids home.' She kisses Victoria. Mum misses us a lot when we go to Dad's. She never asks us what we do with him there. Mum said it's because it hurts her too much. It makes me sad.

Tomorrow I've got to keep my part of the Herman deal. I have to lend Lennie my roller-blades for a whole week. I want to have one last roller-blade. I get them from my room. They're black with purple straps and yellow wheels. I had to save my pocket money for four whole months to buy them. I work for my pocket money. Mum has a list of jobs I have to do. The list's stuck on the fridge.

Jamie's Pocket Money

1. Get dressed for school on time without anyone asking. (Mum thinks I'm a bit slow on account of all the important things I've got to do before school.)
2. Go to bed without discussion. (Mum is really unreasonable at bedtime.)
3. Keep your room tidy. (This is hard if you're an inventor. Mum's pretty understanding, except sometimes she gets mad, like when the glue's stuck to the carpet or she finds the soccer socks I used for last month's match under my bed. It's the smell that turns her off.)

4. Look after Victoria. (I do.)
5. Do homework. (I have to on account of Auntie
Lizzy. You should see how red she gets when I don't.)
$5.00 per week, payable on MONDAY.
(I love Mondays.)

'Mum, can I go and roller-blade before dinner? Just in front of the house. Please. I haven't roller-bladed *all* weekend. Please.' Mum wants to say 'no', because it's getting dark. But she gives in. She always does after we get home from Dad's.

'All right, only for a little while.'

Victoria puts on her roller-skates. They're really my roller-skates, except I grew out of them. She's very good at roller-skating. Not as good as me though. I can do wheelies. 'Move out of the way Victoria, I'm coming.' ZOOM. Like a rocket. I leave white lines on the cement footpath. Wish I didn't have to lend them to Lennie. He's saving for his own roller-blades.

It's hardly been any time at all, when Mum calls us for dinner. 'Kids, come inside now. Dinner is ready.'

Just one last ZOOM. I'm practicing my slide stops. SCREECH. I stop ... 'aaaawh, aaaawh, aaawh ...'

I'm 'aaawhing' for ages. No one comes. I'm lying on the footpath.

'Help,' I cry out. Victoria stands over me. She's no help. At last, Mum's running towards me. I'm yelling.

'It hurts. Hurts. Hurts.'

'What's wrong, Jamie? What's wrong?' I'm moaning. Mum sees it's my arm. She runs into the house, then comes back with ice.

'It'll stop the swelling. It's probably a sprain.'

Now I'm in the back seat of the car. 'Aaawh, aaawh ...' The car jerks. It's killing me. My arm. I shout. Victoria sits on my hand accidentally. I shout very loudly. I'm in too much agony to hit her.

Mum tells her, 'Sit still, Victoria. Jamie's in a lot of pain.'

Victoria says, 'It's not my fault,' and starts crying. Typical.

Mum's upset at all my crying and tells her loudly to, 'Be quiet.'

Hospital. The nurse gives me a sling at the hospital. 'Can I keep it?' The sling is great. The nurse says I can have it. My arm feels a tiny bit better. Then the nurse says I have to have an X-ray. I want an X-ray. I remember having an X-ray when I was four years old. Mum was so angry at me. I was just investigating a five cent coin. 'It's gone,' I'd said to Mum.

'What's gone, Jamie?'

'It's inside now, Mummy.'

'What?'

'The five cents.' Mum looked and looked for the five cents. She couldn't find it.

'I told you Mummy.'

They found the five cents — in my stomach. You

could see a giant black circle in the middle of the X-ray. 'The five cents,' the doctor'd said. 'He should pass it, in the toilet. Come back for an X-ray in two days to see if it's gone through.'

I never found the five cents. But there was no big black circle in the X-ray two days later. The hospital wouldn't let me keep the X-rays, and Mum wouldn't give me another five cents.

Today will only be the third X-ray I've had in my life. The X-ray lady is putting my hand on a special table to take pictures. As an inventor I find the machines very interesting, except it's hard to concentrate when my arm hurts so much. Mum's standing behind a window watching me so she doesn't get radiation from the X-ray machine. She looks upset. After the X-ray, we wait. My hand is throbbing and I'm getting a stomache ache. I'm going to be sick. Victoria wants something to eat. Chocolate. Ugh. At a time like this!

'Broken,' the doctor says, 'at the wrist. In two places.'

Wow. In two places. That's something. I'm impressed with myself. If you're going to break your arm, two breaks is better than one break. I can see the broken lines on the X-ray — my bones. And it's in my right arm. I won't be able to do school work! Excellent. I need a rest from all the extra work I've been doing lately, especially with Auntie Lizzy.

The doctor tells Mum, in a serious voice, 'It'll be

in plaster for four weeks.' I've always wanted a plaster cast.

'Can everyone write on it?'

The doctor rubs the top of my head, 'Yes, after it dries. Tomorrow.'

'I want to be the first to write on it, Jamie.' Mum knows it is an important event in my life. I'm going to keep the cast forever, after it's off my arm of course. Vince had two casts — this will be my first. Maybe I'll break my leg next time. That'd be a giant cast.

Mum asks the doctor, 'What can Jamie do? Will he be able to go to school?'

The doctor looks at me. 'No roller-blading or any sports, Jamie, for six weeks.'

I suppose Lennie can borrow my roller-blades for six weeks now. This is not turning out the way I want.

'You can go to school.' (Horrible!)

This is not turning out the way I want.

'You can write at school with your right hand in a few days time.' (Oh, no. I could've done my inventing with my left hand, who needs my right hand to work?)

This is not turning out the way I want.

Not at all.

Green Frogs and Casts

Dad's angry at Mum because I broke my arm. Strange, isn't it? Mum doesn't even roller-blade. I heard him shout at her on the phone before I went to bed. I can't see why it's Mum's fault. Dad's angry at Mum because she didn't ring him straight away about my broken arm. Mum had enough problems — me in agony and Victoria being a pest. Dad probably would have told Mum off or brought Belinda Chuck-it with him. It would have been awful.

Last night my stomach aches were terrible and I had nightmares. I woke Mum at two am. She opened her eyes a bit, saw it was only me, 'Get in, Jamie, it's cold.' Mum put her arms around me. I felt better straight away. Mum doesn't usually let me or Victoria sleep with her. It's because she says we move and kick her all night and she can't sleep. I can't ever remember doing that. It must be Victoria. But last night she let me sleep with her. I'm so glad because of the enormous giant dark green frogs with men's legs. They kept chasing me through windy streets and creaky stairs and into mucky brown ponds. It's not that I'm a coward or anything. But how would you like *big, ugly frogs* chasing you? The frogs disappeared once I was in Mum's bed. I was so tired. My arm ached.

It's morning and I have to go to school. My school shirt doesn't fit. It's the right sleeve. My arm's stuck halfway up it. How am I supposed to get my shoes on? I can't button up my shorts. Victoria comes into my room. She's watching me. 'Well, what are you staring at, Victoria?'

'You're funny, Jamie.'

I give Victoria a disgusting look and yell out, 'Mum, I need you. Mum. Mum. It's urgent!'

'Stop that shouting, Jamie. What's wrong?' Mum can see what's wrong. I feel my ears going hot and red. But I refuse to cry. Mum smiles. It's a kind smile. I feel my ears getting less red. 'Poor Jamie.' She gets a short sleeved shirt from the cupboard. 'Let's change your shirt. That's better.' I nod. Mum buttons my shorts. Victoria pulls one sock onto my foot and Mum does the other. Mum puts my shoes on my feet. Actually, I hate tying shoelaces. This isn't too bad. I touch my ears with my left hand. They're not hot anymore.

After breakfast, Mum gets out a black felt pen. 'Give me your right arm, Jamie.' Mum thinks for a while: 'First Entry by Mum: To the Roller-blader who rolled with a twist and cracked his wrist just to upset his mother — NO MORE ACCIDENTS JAMIE!' Mum should have been a poet, not an English teacher, don't you think?

Victoria signs her name in giant letters. 'Leave some room for other people,' I tell her.

I can't wait to get to school. Everyone has to sign it. Lennie and Roslyn can write on it first. Even my teacher Mrs Birtwhistle, can sign it. I like her a bit better. She doesn't scream as much, ever since Vince left the school. I think Vince went to gaol or something.

It is an excellent day at school. Firstly, all the kids think it's incredible that I got two breaks, and secondly, they think it's incredible that I got them roller-blading. Joshua only broke his arm falling off a step. Pretty uninteresting. And Timothy just broke his foot falling off his neighbour's garden fence. No one has done anything as good as this.

My cast looks terrific. So far it's got on it: 'Don't kill yourself. Lennie.' (Ha. Ha. As if I would.)

'I really hope your arm is better soon, love Roslyn.' (See, I told you Roslyn was beautiful inside too.)

'Be more careful Jamie, from Mrs Birtwhistle.' (Boring.)

'Cracked rib, next time mate. Joshua.' (Very funny.)

Then it's got lots of names — Luke, Lloyd, Ashley, Carl, Andrew, Robert and Herman. (Lennie put Herman's name on it, since Herman can't write.)

I've left some room on the cast for Auntie Lizzy. I'm going to her place after school for my remedial lesson. I don't mind Auntie Lizzy's lessons anymore. She says I'm getting better. I must be, because it's not so hard to listen to Mrs Birtwhistle these days. And last week, I wrote a great story in class about my inventing. Mrs Birtwhistle gave me an 'A'. I've never, ever got an 'A' before.

After school Victoria and I walk with Lennie and Roslyn to their house. I'm getting pretty tired dragging my school bag there. I have my roller-blades in my bag. It's Monday, and a promise is a promise. Instead of me holding my soccer ball, Victoria and Roslyn bounce it on the footpath. I suppose that's a help. The roller-blades are too heavy. I drop my bag. Lennie can have them *now*. We're at the bottom of his street anyway. Auntie Lizzy has got funny about roller-blading too far from home. She thinks everyone's going to break an arm or leg. I can't see why it matters where you are when you break it.

Lennie's fast. His shoes are off and the roller-blades are on. 'Thanks, Jamie,' he calls out, roller-blading up the street. He'll be home way before me.

Auntie Lizzy has some fruit cut up on a plate for us kids and some drinks. Roslyn's already eating a pear. It's dripping down the corners of her mouth. Horrible. Victoria's drinking lemonade and I'm starving.

'Ready to work, Jamie?' I can't answer because a starving boy has to eat. I gulp down a mouthful of apple. 'All right, finish eating.' Auntie Lizzy smiles. 'Then you can go to the desk and start working.' 'Play outside. Jamie needs some quiet,' she says to everyone else. I feel important.

Through the window, I can see Lennie whizzing up and down the driveway on my roller-blades. I only feel a tiny bit jealous. I have to give him my second best rock afterwards. It's in my pocket. Roslyn and Victoria are calling out. 'You're good, Lennie. Faster, Lennie.' They're laughing while I get to write out a spelling list with my *left* hand. Auntie Lizzy has found the white spot I left on my cast for her. She has a red felt pen and is concentrating, while I'm spelling. Then she writes:

Roses are red
nephews are blue
especially Jamie,
when he lands in the POO.
Love from Lizzy.

That's funny. But Auntie Lizzy IS rude.

Uncle Tom's Birthday

I'm getting used to my cast. It's very practical. I've already flattened a soccer ball with it. (The soccer ball was wrecked anyway.) Kids are afraid of my arm. I just swing it at them and they know. Come near me and they'll get clobbered. I'm the secret weapon when we're playing battles or sword fights or handball. (I don't tell Mum I do that. What's the point of upsetting her?)

Tonight Uncle Tom and my *big* cousins are coming over. It's for Uncle Tom's birthday. He says he's twenty-one. I think he's not telling the truth because my *biggest* cousin Debbie, is eighteen. That would mean Uncle Tom was a dad when he was three years old! I bet he's at least thirty-one.

Yesterday my mum baked a chocolate cake and put on twenty-one candles. Mum wrote on Uncle Tom's birthday card:

'To my dearest brother Tom,
Thanks for all your support during this divorce.
Thanks for being there for my children.

Thanks for being the same big brother.
You're always 21 to me!
Love from your sister.'

I drew a picture of a dog (I'm good at that) and signed my name in giant letters — J A M I E. Victoria drew a clown and wrote her name in a blue coloured pencil. We bought Uncle Tom his favourite things — socks (two pairs), a blue-striped shirt, a dark blue tie and a pair of bright red spotted underpants. Victoria picked the underpants, but she wanted to buy *pink* ones. Mum said, 'NO, red spotted underpants are colourful enough.' I hope no one gives me underpants for my birthday!

My big cousins are Debbie (I mentioned her already), and Lisa (she's sixteen) and Paul (he's fifteen). They're the best. I go fishing with my cousin Paul, and Lisa jumps on the trampoline with me and Debbie gives me muesli bars to eat. I love my cousins. Their mum is the best too. She's very good at sewing. She made Victoria a princess dress. It was all white lace with silver and gold in it and Victoria had a crown too. I hate to say this, but Victoria really did look like a beautiful princess.

'They're here. They're here!' Victoria runs as fast as she can into Uncle Tom's arms. He picks her up and she clings onto him like a koala bear.

Everyone's impressed with my broken arm. My big cousin Paul broke his arm once, when he fell off a horse. His horse bolted when another horse bit its bottom. Pretty funny. Everyone signs the cast. Then I drag my big cousin Paul, into my bedroom to see Herman. And my invention.

By the way I've got used to Herman's croaks. I really like Herman. You know, if I didn't have school work and Auntie Lizzy's work and having to help Mum and going to see Dad every weekend and minding Victoria, I'd have finished my invention by now. But it's all right. Everyone has things they've got to do.

Paul's amazed by my invention. In the middle of saying, 'It's fantastic, Jamie', there're these big screams. We run out of the bedroom. Guess what? Victoria's running around the lounge room in Uncle Tom's new *red* spotted underpants. They're enormous. Everyone's laughing. My big cousin Debbie grabs Victoria around her waist and swings her around. The red spotted pants fall off and Mum gets them. She throws the underpants to Uncle Tom, 'I think they'd look better on you.'

We sing 'Happy Birthday' to Uncle Tom. He lets Victoria blow out his candles. She hasn't that much puff, so I help her blow. It is my job to look after her. Is she grateful? NO. She whinges. 'You blew out the candles, Jamie. It's not fair ...' She makes so much noise that Mum has to light the twenty-one candles again. Poor Mum. Victoria still can't blow them all out. Uncle Tom helps her. She doesn't mind that and hugs him. Typical.

The cake is delicious. I have two pieces. Victoria's eating her cake sitting in Uncle Tom's lap. Then Uncle Tom calls my mum. 'Could you look at this? He points to Victoria's head. Mum looks really hard at Victoria's head. Then nods. 'Later,' she says to Uncle Tom.

The birthday is great fun. But *later* is right. When they've gone, Mum inspects Victoria's head again. Victoria's head is ALIVE! I race to get a jar. I'm going to catch some and put them under my microscope. 'Stop it, Jamie. Stop it.' I keep squashing them every time I find one. Then there's nothing left to look at. I've got a lot of eggs though. There's hundreds of them. 'Stop moving, Victoria.' Caught two live ones. Excellent. Mum's brought out a bottle with POISON S2 written on it. 'You can go first Jamie.'

'Me? Why me? I've nothing alive on my head.'

'Jamie, everyone has to get treated, unless you want to have them too.'

The poison stinks! Mum rubs this disgusting stuff into my hair. Then she does it to Victoria. Then Mum does it to herself. We're all standing there with our hair sticking straight up into the air, looking like electrocuted glue balls. What a way to end a birthday party!

Mum stares at me. I stare at Mum. Victoria stares at us both. We start giggling and giggling and ... it's not funny. It's really, truly not funny. But us nuts have got ... you know what? NITS.

Nits and Belinda Chuck-it

Dad says Mum's hopeless, just because Victoria's got nits. I tried to tell Dad that Mum already washed our hair. And that Mum spent hours and hours pulling the white eggs out of Victoria's hair afterwards. Dad wouldn't listen. Belinda Chuck-it just shook her head trying to say Mum's stupid. As if Belinda Chuck-it would know. She doesn't even have any kids or ... nits. Until now, that is.

Dad bought some more POISON S2. We got another nit treatment. Dad made Belinda Chuck-it have it too. That was the best part. She's got long hair, and when all the stuff was in her hair she looked beyond belief. UGLY. Poor Dad.

'Come on, Jamie. After all this, we deserve some fish and chips for dinner. What do you want Victoria?'

'Daddy, I want chips and scallops. And can I go with you?'

Dad looks at Victoria. 'You're in pyjamas and

your head's wet. No, you'll catch a cold. Anyway Belinda wants the company. She likes you a lot. We'll be back soon.'

I'm glad I'm wearing a tracksuit. Who'd want to stay with *her*? I feel a bit rotten about leaving Victoria, but it is good for her to look after herself sometimes.

Dad and I are already out of the door. I can hear Victoria calling out, 'I don't want to stay with her. Let me come.'

We go to our favourite fish and chip shop. It's got prawns and crabs and lobsters in the window. The fish and chip man is Hungarian. He talks very loudly and I can just see him smile under an enormous moustache. I think I'll grow a moustache when I'm older. He likes me. 'Chips and prawns for you?' He winks. 'You'll need a few more prawns Jamie, for a big boy.' I stretch a bit. I'm pretty tall. I love prawns. The fish and chip man always puts in a few extra ones for free.

The fish and chips smell delicious. But Dad says we have to wait till we get home to eat them. 'Hurry up, Dad, I'm hungry.' Dad drives fast.

In the car, I tell Dad all about my invention. 'It's finished. I'm going to show it to you and Mum and everyone on Open Day at school.'

Mum and Dad probably won't talk to each other at Open Day. Auntie Lizzy and Uncle Tom won't talk to Dad either. All this makes me feel sort of sick inside. I hope Dad doesn't bring Belinda Chuck-it.

But I want Mum and Dad, Auntie Lizzy and Lennie and Roslyn and Uncle Tom and all of them to come.

'Everyone in the class had a project to do. A few of the kids did some pottery which wasn't bad. Lots of them drew posters and a few made models. Joshua made a model of a battleship out of matchsticks.' Dad looks interested. I'm taking my invention to school, only on Open Day on account of Herman. Dad shouldn't mind Herman anymore. There's prizes for the best projects. I hope mine's one of the best.

We're at the unit at last. Dad opens the front door and I put the fish and chips on the table. We can't see Belinda Chuck-it or Victoria. Oh, they're in the bedroom. I can hear Belinda Chuck-it's voice.

'I really think you and your brother are awful to me, and your mother is awful too.' There's dead silence. Dad's standing in the bedroom doorway. I'm behind him. We don't move. Belinda Chuck-it can't see us.

Victoria is looking at the floor. She's crying quietly.

'Why are you so mean to me? What have I done?' Victoria looks at the doorway and sees us. She runs into Dad's arms. I stroke her arm. I shouldn't have left Victoria. Jamie's no hero now, I know.

Belinda Chuck-it goes really white. Her nose looks gigantic. 'It was just a little argument over ...' Belinda Chuck-it coughs twice. 'Victoria and I are friends. It was nothing.'

She's such a liar. Even Dad couldn't lie like this.

Belinda Chuck-it's still talking. 'You get angry at the children sometimes, don't you?'

Yeh, but Dad would never, ever even think for a tiny, little bit, that we were awful.

Dad has an angry look in his eyes. He doesn't say anything to Belinda Chuck-it. We eat fish and chips at the table. Victoria's sitting in Dad's lap eating chips. She's put so much tomato sauce on the chips you can't see them. I don't even think it's disgusting. I'm just happy Victoria is with Dad and me. Dad's eating the fish. He nearly chokes on a bone. Belinda Chuck-it is eating fish too. She doesn't choke. I can only eat one prawn because my stomach is hurting so much.

Open Day

This is Lennie's last year at primary school. Next year is high school. I'll miss him when he leaves. His class is putting on a final year play for Open Day. Lennie's got a major part.

Oh, NO. Lennie's coming onto the stage. He looks revolting. I don't mind the huge black wig he's got on, or the big white bra with tennis balls in it. It's the giant wart he's stuck on his nose with three long hairs coming out of it. (I think he got the wart at the Magic Shop.)

Auntie Lizzy's laughing so much she nearly falls off the chair. Victoria keeps pointing at Lennie's nose.

'Will it come off? Will it? Will it?' Victoria's very upset. Mum calms her down.

'It's only a pretend wart, Victoria.' Victoria starts laughing too. Then Roslyn starts laughing, then Mum does. I control myself, mainly because I'm worried about my invention.

I left Herman and my invention in the Staff Room with Mrs Birtwhistle. Nobody had better touch it.

Lennie's giving Cinderella a bad time. So you've guessed, Lennie's one of the ugly sisters in 'Cinderella'. It's a cracked fairytale. It sure is cracked. Lennie's going to break a leg walking around in his mum's high heels. Then he can have a plaster cast too. I'd be so embarrassed wearing a bra, if I was Lennie.

I'm on after Lennie and the choir. In my play, I'm in charge of the drums. Every time there's a new character on the stage, I bang these drums. It's a very important role Mrs Birtwhistle says. It's because if I drum roll wrongly, the characters will be in the wrong places. Having a broken arm actually helps. When I need a very loud sound, I bang my cast on the drums.

Victoria and Roslyn are in the choir. They've been practising a song about a lion, ALL DAY, ALL WEEK, ALL TERM. It's been driving me crazy!

My dad's arrived. Am I supposed to go up to him? Will I hurt Mum's feelings? Maybe Auntie Lizzy will be angry if I talk to him. What'll I do? I don't feel very hero-like. I'm ... scared.

Dad's waving at me. There's no Belinda Chuck-it, thank goodness. Mum sees Dad. 'Jamie, it's all right. Go and sit with your father.' I love my mum. 'Victoria, you go with Jamie.'

Dad sits in the middle of the hall. We watch 'Cinderella' with him. Victoria is on Dad's lap. Prince Charming has found Cinderella. She's making afternoon tea for the two Ugly Sisters as well as Prince Charming. Prince Charming looks at Cinderella and

asks, 'Can I have some sugar? SUGAR.' Prince
Charming looks at Cinderella and asks, 'Can I have
some honey? HONEY.' Prince Charming looks at
Lennie, the Ugly Sister, 'Can I have some tea? BAG.'
Everyone laughs. Dad does too. I sort of laugh, but I
feel funny about Mum and everyone else sitting on the
other side of the hall.

Victoria and Roslyn join the choir. They have a
lion mask that they keep putting in front of their
faces when they roar. And would you believe it?
They have an orange lion's tail pinned to their
school uniforms. Victoria flicks the tail into Roslyn's
face. Roslyn just ignores her. Roslyn's a very nice
person really. I hope this means I won't have to hear
that stupid lion song again.

I'm needed. My play's on next. 'Got to go, Dad.'
He wants Victoria to stay with him, but she goes
back to Mum. I think that's better.

My class play is 'Jack and The Beanstalk'. The
drum rolling was perfect, Mrs Birtwhistle says. I
really wanted to be the stage manager and organise
all the props, but Joshua got picked for that. Still,
drum rolling is a very responsible job.

After our play Mrs Birtwhistle gets onto the stage.
'I would like to invite all the parents and friends and
children to see the project competition to be held in
my classroom. It will be on in fifteen minutes.'

Urgent. I run around like a maniac to find Lennie.
He's in his classroom, just taking off his wart.

'Lennie, please I need you NOW. Hurry.'

Lennie is a great cousin. He doesn't even ask me why. He quickly puts his wart in his bag with his wig and high heels and bra and dress. Then he points at the door. 'Let's go, Jamie.'

Mrs Birtwhistle isn't in the Staff Room. Another teacher lets us get my invention. We carry Herman and my invention under a sheet (so no one can see) to my classroom.

Parents and kids are sitting on desks and school chairs listening to Joshua explain how he made his battleship. It is very good. He'll get a prize for sure.

Roslyn and Victoria have come up to see what's under the sheet. 'Leave it alone,' I tell them. I'm getting nervous. Four kids are showing their pottery. One isn't too bad. It's a brown clay snake with its head stuck in the air. But it's not as good as Joshua's battleship.

Mrs Birtwhistle annouces. 'Jamie has been working on his project all term.' She turns to me. 'Would you like to show the parents and friends what you've done?'

Lennie helps me put it on Mrs Birtwhistle's desk. Uncle Tom's just walked into the room. That makes me feel a bit nervous. Hope he likes it. He's standing behind Mum and Auntie Lizzy. Dad's watching. He'll probably think it's stupid, because he's an engineer and knows how to invent.

'Come on,' Lennie whispers. We take off the

sheet. There's this 'oooohhhh' sound coming from the audience. Herman croaks.

'This boy is special,' I hear someone say. (Me! I've never been special before.) 'It's incredible.' (They're talking about my invention!)

Herman is a star. He jumps on the paddle-pop stick pad I'd attached to a lever that pushes a ball. Everyone watches the ball circle and circle. It goes around the whole paddle-pop stick building twice. The paddle-pop stick building is about 45 centimetres high. Taller than my ruler. So you can understand why it took me so long to make. The ball lands in a hole that starts the battery switch. There's a zip from the circuit. I loved making the circuit. There's wires and lights attached to the battery. Red and yellow lights are flashing. I didn't have time to get blue ones too. The battery Victoria squashed is working very well! The power from my electric circuit throws the ball into the small pool of water in the paddle-pop stick structure. Herman jumps into the pool with a splash right on top of the ball. Then it starts again. Herman's splash pops the ball onto the paddle-pop stick pad. The pad and the lever under it is halfway in the pond. Herman jumps again onto the ball and off it goes. My uncle Tom is clapping. My dad is too. Mum and Auntie Lizzy and Roslyn and Victoria and Lennie are clapping. The clapping goes on and on.

Lennie grabs my arm. 'You're a great inventor, Jamie. You deserve Herman. He's yours.'

Jamie's Famous

Herman and my invention are on display next to the Headmistress' Office. It has a sign on it — 'FIRST PRIZE' Project Competition. I'm famous now.

Last night Mum checked our heads. No more nits *and* I didn't have any nightmares. I had a great dream about being an outstanding inventor. I didn't even have to ask Mum to help me go to sleep. Maybe I'm getting braver.

It's not Saturday, but Dad's taking Victoria and me out for dinner tonight. It's because Dad's so proud of me. Mum said Dad could take us out, as long as we're home by eight o'clock.

'Tomorrow's a school day, kids. You've got to go to bed on time.' If you ask me, Mum's got a real problem about us going to bed. I'd like to stay up at least until ten o'clock like Dad lets us.

Dad's beeping the horn in his four-wheel drive. We run out of the house. *She's* not in the car. Excellent.

'Hi, inventor,' Dad smiles. 'Come in kids, we're

celebrating at "No Names, the Spaghetti House".'
Great! My favourite.

'Daddy, I've got no more nits and can I have
noodles? Please,' Victoria squeaks.

'What do you think you eat at a spaghetti place?
Honestly, Victoria you're dumb.'

'Daddy, Jamie called me dumb. I'm not. I just
want spaghetti.'

'It's all right, Victoria. Jamie, you're getting a big
mouth. Keep quiet and don't tease your sister.'

I want to argue, but I notice a a huge crane lifting
bricks onto a three storey house. It's more exciting
than Victoria's noodles.

'Dad, look.' Dad only sights the crane for a few
seconds, because he's driving. Then he explains how
a crane works. It has an interesting mechanical
engine. This is giving me ideas for my next project.
We're there. 'No Names' is full. We have to wait for
a table. Then we get the best table. It's on the
balcony overlooking the street. I'm making a paper
aeroplane out of my serviette so that I can fly it off
the balcony after dinner. I order a giant bowl of
spaghetti bolognaise. Dad orders a tiny bowl for
Victoria because she never eats much. She just asks
for lots of food. Her eyes are much bigger than her
stomach. Dad gets ravioli. There's crunchy Italian
bread. I butter two slices for myself. Dad butters one
slice for Victoria. This is delicious.

In between mouthfuls I tell Dad, 'It's great going

out with just us three.' I don't like to say anything about *her* in case Dad gets mad at me. I don't know if I'm supposed to still like her, after what she said to Victoria.

'Yes, it's nice to be together. Belinda and I have to work out a few things. It's fine with just the three of us.' Dad rubs my hair. Good, good, good, I keep thinking. I take a deep breath.

'Maybe, Mum can come with us instead.'

Dad shakes his head. 'Sometimes things are broken and there's no way to fix them. That's what's happened between your mother and me. It's not like your broken arm. By the way, when will your cast be taken off?'

'Next week, Dad.' We talk about my arm for a while. I can't wait to start roller-blading again. Lennie'll have to give my roller-blades back. He's saved money to buy his own now, anyway. I throw my serviette paper plane off the balcony. Victoria's impressed. It goes right across the other side of the street.

Dad says, 'No more planes, Jamie.'

'Just one more for Victoria. Please,' I beg.

'All right. But only *one* more plane. The waiters won't like it.' I start making a paper plane for Victoria.

Dad holds Victoria's hand. 'You know, Victoria, you, Jamie and I are going to have fun together.'

'We do Dad,' I answer back.

'Do you kids want to go to the Science Museum on Sunday?' Victoria nods her head.

I'm excited. 'Yes, Dad.' We talk about all the experiments we'll see at the museum. 'There's a great rock and mineral exhibition there too, Dad.' I give Victoria the plane. She throws it straight down and hits a man on the head. Luckily he's not hurt. It is only a serviette. Dad shouts down, 'Sorry'.

When will Victoria not get into trouble? It's hard work being her brother. I look at Dad, and I sort of know that Mum and Dad won't get back together again. It makes me sad, but I feel like a big knot is slowly coming undone in my stomach. Inside me, I know I'm luckier than a lot of other kids because I have Lennie and Roslyn and Auntie Lizzy and Uncle Tom. There're my *big* cousins and Victoria who's a princess, sometimes. (Really, I don't mind taking care of Victoria. She is MY sister.) And I know my mum loves me the best in the world. She's said so lots of times.

School work is easier, though I still don't like it too much. I'll never be as smart as Lennie at it. But I know everything is sort of all right. I feel brave, like a hero. Maybe I can't have my dad at home. Maybe I can't have a mum and dad who talk to each other. But Mum won't leave me and Victoria. Dad'll be there for me and Victoria too.

And I have Herman. I like him. You know, I'm not so scared.

Dad drops us off at eight-thirty. Mum's standing at the front door, annoyed. She's pointing to her watch. 'Late,' she's calling out. We wave to Dad driving off. Mum kisses us.

'Good, to have you kids home.'

Yep, I'm glad we're home.